BEDTIME
STORIES

Illustrated by

GUSTAF TENGGREN

A GOLDEN BOOK • NEW YORK

Western Publishing Company, Inc.
Racine, Wisconsin 53404

THE LITTLE GOLDEN BOOKS
ARE PREPARED UNDER THE SUPERVISION OF
MARY REED, Ph.D.
ASSISTANT PROFESSOR OF EDUCATION
TEACHERS COLLEGE, COLUMBIA UNIVERSITY

A COMMEMORATIVE FACSIMILE EDITION PUBLISHED ON THE OCCASION OF
THE 50TH ANNIVERSARY OF LITTLE GOLDEN BOOKS

Chicken Little

ONE DAY Chicken Little strutted through
the woods on her way to market. A tiny acorn
fell from a tall tree and hit the top of her little
head.

"My goodness! The sky is falling!" said Chicken Little. "I must rush to tell the King!"

Chicken Little met Henny Penny on the path.

"Where are you going?" asked Henny Penny.

"The sky is falling," said Chicken Little. "I'm off to tell the King."

"Who told you?" asked Henny Penny.

"It hit me on the head," said Chicken Little.

"Let me come with you," said Henny Penny.

And Chicken Little and Henny Penny hurried

off to tell the King. On the way they met Ducky Lucky.

"Where are you going?" asked Ducky Lucky.

"The sky is falling," said Henny Penny. "We're off to tell the King."

"Who told you?" asked Ducky Lucky.

"Chicken Little."

"Who told Chicken Little?"

"It hit her on the head."

"Let me come with you," said Ducky Lucky.

And Chicken Little, Henny Penny, and Ducky Lucky hurried off to tell the King. On the way they met Goosey Loosey.

"Where are you going?" asked Goosey Loosey.

"The sky is falling," said Ducky Lucky. "We're off to tell the King."

"Who told you?" asked Goosey Loosey.

"Henny Penny."

"Who told Henny Penny?"

"Chicken Little."

"Who told Chicken Little?"

"It hit her on the head."

"Let me come with you," said Goosey Loosey.

And Chicken Little, Henny Penny, Ducky Lucky, and Goosey Loosey hurried off to tell the King. On the way they met Turkey Lurkey.

"Where are you going?" asked Turkey Lurkey.
"The sky is falling," said Goosey Loosey. "We're
off to tell the King."

"Who told you?" asked Turkey Lurkey.

"Ducky Lucky."

"Who told Ducky Lucky?"

"Henny Penny."

"Who told Henny Penny?"

"Chicken Little."

"Who told Chicken Little?"

"It hit her on the head."

"Let me come with you," said Turkey Lurkey.

So Chicken Little and Henny Penny and Ducky Lucky and Goosey Loosey and Turkey Lurkey hurried off to tell the King the sky was falling. And on the way they met Foxy Loxy.

"Where are you going?" asked Foxy Loxy.

"The sky is falling. We're off to tell the King."

"Let me show you the way," said Foxy Loxy.

Then Foxy Loxy walked with Turkey Lurkey.

Foxy Loxy ate Turkey Lurkey.

Foxy Loxy walked with Goosey Loosey.

Foxy Loxy ate Goosey Loosey.

Foxy Loxy walked with Ducky Lucky.

Foxy Loxy ate Ducky Lucky.

Foxy Loxy walked with Henny Penny.

Foxy Loxy ate Henny Penny.

Foxy Loxy walked with Chicken Little.

Foxy Loxy ate Chicken Little.

And there was no one left to tell the King but Foxy Loxy himself.

But Foxy Loxy was much too full to move.

So the King never knew that the sky was falling.

The Three Bears

ONE DAY a great big Papa Bear and a middle-sized Mama Bear and a wee little Baby Bear went

for a walk in the woods. They left their bowls of porridge to cool on the table.

A little girl called Goldilocks walked by the house, and the wonderful smell of porridge floated out to her.

"M-m-m-m-m," said Goldilocks. "That smells good!" And she hurried into the little house.

She tasted the porridge of the great big Papa Bear, but it was too hot.

She tasted the porridge of the middle-sized Mama Bear, but it was too cold.

She tasted the porridge of the wee little Baby

Bear—and it was just right. So she ate it all up.

Goldilocks was very tired. She saw three chairs near the table.

She sat in the chair of the great big Papa Bear, but it was too hard.

She sat in the chair of the middle-sized Mama Bear, but it was too soft.

She sat in the chair of the wee little Baby Bear—and it was just right. So she rocked and rocked and rocked in the chair till it broke into many pieces.

Then Goldilocks was very sleepy. She went upstairs, and there she saw three beds.

She tried to take a nap in the bed of the great big Papa Bear, but it was too hard.

So she tried to take a nap in the bed of the middle-sized Mama Bear, but it was too soft.

And then she tried the bed of the wee little Baby Bear—and it was just right. Soon Goldilocks was fast asleep.

The great big Papa Bear and the middle-sized Mama Bear and the wee little Baby Bear came home from their walk. They were very hungry, and they went right to the bowls of porridge on the table.

"SOMEBODY'S BEEN TASTING MY POR-RIDGE!" cried the great big Papa Bear in a great big voice.

"Somebody's been tasting my porridge!" cried the middle-sized Mama Bear in a middle-sized voice.

"Somebody's been tasting my porridge—and has eaten it all up!" cried the wee little Baby Bear in a wee little voice.

The great big Papa Bear and the middle-sized Mama Bear and the wee little Baby Bear were very tired. They looked at their chairs.

"SOMEBODY'S BEEN SITTING IN MY CHAIR!" cried the great big Papa Bear in a great big voice.

"Somebody's been sitting in my chair!" cried the middle-sized Mama Bear in a middle-sized voice.

"Somebody's been sitting in my chair—and has broken it into pieces!" cried the wee little Baby Bear in a wee little voice.

All this made the great big Papa Bear and the middle-sized Mama Bear and the wee little Baby Bear very sleepy. They went upstairs.

"SOMEBODY'S BEEN SLEEPING IN MY BED!" thundered the great big Papa Bear in a great big voice.

"Somebody's been sleeping in my bed!" called the middle-sized Mama Bear in a middle-sized voice.

"Somebody's been sleeping in my bed—and here she is!" cried the wee little Baby Bear.

And the three Bears stood around the bed on which Goldilocks was sleeping, and looked at her.

Then Goldilocks woke up! She was so surprised when she saw the three Bears that she rushed down the stairs and out of the door and ran all the way home.

And she never went near the Bears' little house again.

The Three Little Pigs

ONE DAY three little pigs started out to seek
their fortunes.

"Take care of yourselves," said their mother as
she waved a tearful good-by, "and beware of the
Wolf."

The Oldest Little Pig met a man who gave
him some straw to build himself a house. And the
pig built himself a little straw house.

One day the Wolf trotted up to the little straw house.

"Little pig, little pig, let me in, let me in!" he snarled.

"Not by the hair of my chinny, chin, chin!" cried the pig.

"Then I'll huff and I'll puff till I blow your house in," roared the Wolf.

So he huffed and he puffed till he blew the house in. Then he ate up the Oldest Little Pig.

The Second Little Pig met another man, who gave him some sticks to build himself a house. And the Second Pig built a little house of sticks.

One day the Wolf trotted up to the little house of sticks.

"Little pig, little pig, let me in, let me in!" he snarled.

"Not by the hair of my chinny, chin, chin!" cried the pig.

"Then I'll huff and I'll puff till I blow your house in," roared the Wolf.

So he huffed and he puffed till he blew the house in. Then he ate up the Second Little Pig.

The Little Baby Pig met still another man, who gave him some bricks to build himself a house. And the Baby Pig built himself a little house of bricks.

One day the Wolf trotted up to the little brick house.

"Little pig, little pig, let me in, let me in!" he snarled.

"Not by the hair of my chinny, chin, chin!" cried the Little Baby Pig.

"Then I'll huff and I'll puff till I blow your house in," roared the Wolf.

And he huffed and he puffed and he puffed and he huffed but he couldn't blow the house in.

The Wolf was very angry, but he said slyly:

"Little pig, little pig, meet me in the orchard before breakfast tomorrow, and I'll show you some wonderful red apples."

"I'll be there," said the Little Baby Pig.

But when the Wolf came to the orchard the next morning, the Little Baby Pig was high up in the apple tree.

"Bring me an apple," coaxed the Wolf, licking his chops.

"Here!" cried the Little Baby Pig, and he threw down a beautiful red apple. But the apple started rolling down the hill. Round and round and round it rolled. Then while the Wolf was chasing after it, the Little Baby Pig jumped out of the tree and ran and ran all the way home.

The next day the Little Baby Pig went to the fair to buy a churn.

On the way home, he met the Wolf—waiting to eat him!

But the Little Baby Pig climbed into the churn and rolled and rolled all the way home. And the Wolf was so frightened by the strange sight that he ran home, too.

The next day, the Wolf came to the Little Baby Pig's house again and climbed up onto the roof.

"Little pig, little pig," he growled, "I'm coming down the chimney to eat you!"

"Come ahead," said the Little Baby Pig, who had a big pot of water on the fire.

Down the chimney slid the Wolf—and landed, with a hiss and a splash, right in the pot of boiling water.

That was the end of the Wolf, and the Little Baby Pig lived happily ever after in his little brick house.

Little Red Riding Hood

ONCE there was a little girl who was called Red Riding Hood because of her pretty red cloak.

One day her mother put some gingerbread and a jar of butter into a basket and said to her, "Take this basket to your grandmother, and don't talk to strangers on the way."

On the way through the woods, Little Red Riding Hood was so busy watching the birds and picking flowers that she forgot her mother's warning. Suddenly—

"Hello," said a deep, gruff voice. And there was a big black Wolf.

"Where are you going, little girl?" asked the Wolf, putting on his best manners.

"To my grandmother's," said Little Red Riding Hood, "to take her this basket."

"I'd like to go too," said the Wolf, smacking his lips. "You take the path by the brook and I'll take the path by the spring, and we'll see who gets there first."

The Wolf ran and ran and ran, and reached the grandmother's house long before Little Red Riding Hood.

"Tap-tap," went the Wolf's paw on the door.

"Come in, Little Red Riding Hood," said the grandmother.

But it wasn't Little Red Riding Hood who trotted in. It was the big black Wolf!

The grandmother ran into the closet and locked the door.

Then the Wolf dressed up in Grandmother's nightdress and nightcap, and climbed into Grandmother's bed.

At last Little Red Riding Hood reached the little house.

"Tap-tap," went the little girl's hand on the door.

"Come in, Little Red Riding Hood," said a gruff voice in the house.

Little Red Riding Hood went in and saw her grandmother in night clothes and nightcap in bed. She thought her grandmother looked very strange.

"Oh, Grandmother, what big eyes you have!" said Little Red Riding Hood.

"The better to see you, my dear."

"And Grandmother, what big ears you have!"

"The better to hear you, my dear."

"And Grandmother, what big teeth you have!"

"The better to EAT you, my dear," snarled the Wolf, jumping out of bed.

"O-o-o-o-h," screamed Little Red Riding Hood.

A hunter, passing by, heard her and rushed into the house. He shot the Wolf with his gun.

"Grandmother, Grandmother," called Little Red Riding Hood.

"Here I am," said her grandmother, coming out of the closet.

"And here is the basket I brought you," said Little Red Riding Hood.

Then Grandmother kissed Little Red Riding Hood and gave the hunter some gingerbread.

But from that day on, Little Red Riding Hood never again stopped to talk to strangers on her way to her grandmother's house.

The Gingerbread Man

ONCE UPON a time a little old man and a little old woman lived together in a little wooden house near the edge of the forest.

One day the little old woman decided to bake some goodies for the little old man, who loved anything sweet. So she baked cookies and cakes— and a beautiful gingerbread man! He had raisins for eyes, currants for his mouth and nose, and pink sugar-candies for buttons. When he was done, the little old woman took him out of the oven, put him on the window sill to cool, and went out in the garden to sweep off the paths.

As soon as she was out of sight, the gingerbread man sat up, peeked around, and stepped out on the table. He climbed down to the floor, skipped over to the door, and looked out. He saw that the road was clear, so he ran out the door and down the path.

But as he ran, the little old woman saw him and cried, "Stop! Stop!"

But the gingerbread man laughed and answered, "Run, run as fast as you can, you can't catch me. I'm the Gingerbread Man!" And with that he ran even faster, with the little old woman running behind him.

Soon they came to the field where the little old man was planting cabbages. When he saw the gingerbread man running away and the little old woman trying to catch him, he cried out, "Stop! Stop!"

But the gingerbread man called back, "Run, run as fast as you can, you can't catch me. I'm the Gingerbread Man! I got away from the little old woman, and I can get away from you, I can, I can." And with that he ran even faster, with the little old woman and the little old man running behind him.

Soon they came to a clover patch where a big white rabbit was nibbling the clover flowers. When the rabbit saw the tasty gingerbread man, he thought how good he would taste after a meal of clover. So he cried, "Stop! Stop!"

But the gingerbread man laughed and cried out,

"Run, run as fast as you can, you can't catch me. I'm the Gingerbread Man! I got away from the little old woman and the little old man, and I can get away from you, I can, I can." And with that he ran even faster, with the little old woman, the little old man, and the big white rabbit running after him.

Next they came to a pasture where a gentle brown cow was chewing her cud. When she saw the delicious gingerbread man running down the road, she thought of how much better it would be to eat a gingerbread man than to chew her cud, so she cried, "Stop! Stop!"

But the gingerbread man laughed and cried, "Run, run as fast as you can, you can't catch me. I'm the Gingerbread Man! I got away from the little old woman, the little old man, and a big white rabbit, and I can get away from you, I can, I can." And with that he ran even faster, with the little old woman, the little old man, the big white rabbit, and the gentle brown cow after him.

Soon they came to a honey tree, where a little bear cub was eating the honey. When the little bear smelled the wonderful gingerbread man, he thought how good gingerbread would taste right after a meal of honey. So the little bear cried, "Stop! Stop!"

But the gingerbread man laughed and cried, "Run, run as fast as you can, you can't catch me. I'm the Gingerbread Man! I got away from the little old woman, the little old man, the big white rabbit, and the gentle brown cow, and I can get away from you, I can, I can." And with that he ran a little bit faster, with the little old woman, the little old man, the big white rabbit, the gentle brown cow, and the little bear cub running after him.

The gingerbread man was getting tired now, but he would not give up. And when he saw a workingman eating his lunch under the tree, he knew he would have to run even faster. The workingman took one look at that delicious gingerbread man, and decided that gingerbread was just what he wanted for his dessert, so he cried out, "Stop! Stop!"

But the gingerbread man got his second wind

and laughed, and cried out, "Run, run as fast as you can, you can't catch me. I'm the Gingerbread Man! I got away from the little old woman, the little old man, the big white rabbit, the gentle brown cow, and the little bear cub, and I can get away from you, I can, I can." And on he ran with the little old woman, the little old man, the big white rabbit, the gentle brown cow, the little bear

cub, and the workingman all running after him.

On and on they all ran, along the paths, through the fields and over the hills. Soon the gingerbread man saw a river before him, and he did not know how he could cross it. But a wily red fox was sitting near the river, and when he saw the gingerbread man, he decided that he would eat him.

As the gingerbread man ran up to the river, the wily red fox ran out to meet him.

"Jump on my tail and I will carry you across the river," he called to the gingerbread man.

"If I do, you will eat me," said the gingerbread man.

"Oh, no!" declared the fox. "I don't like gingerbread."

So the gingerbread man jumped on the fox's tail, and the fox waded into the river. But soon the water grew so deep that it lapped about the toes of the gingerbread man.

"Jump on my back!" cried the wily red fox.

The gingerbread man jumped on the fox's back, but soon the water lapped about the gingerbread man's feet.

"Jump on my head," cried the fox.

The gingerbread man jumped on the fox's head, but soon the water lapped about the gingerbread man's feet.

"Jump on my nose," said the wily red fox.

The gingerbread man jumped on the fox's nose, but as soon as he did the fox snapped him up and ate him.

And that is just what should happen to all gingerbread men!